On The Edge:

Transitioning Imaginatively to College

By Eric Bierker Ph.D.

THIS BOOK IS DEDICATED TO MRS. MAYNARD.
MY 2ND GRADE TEACHER. YOU STILL WALK WITH ME.

Table of Contents

10% of the proceeds of this book will be donated to the American Indian College Fund where
Education = Hope
www.collegefund.org

Introduction - Imagination

The power of our imagination makes us infinite.
John Muir

When writing this book over a three year period on Saturdays, I envisioned it to be in the spirit of Jack Kerouac's quote from his epic book *On the Road* where he wrote, "I was halfway across America, at the dividing line between the East of my youth and the West of my future."

For many emerging adults this dividing line between youth and their adult future is the college campus. I have served students for twenty-five years as a teacher, counselor to college freshman, and a high school guidance counselor, preparing them for the next critical steps of college. During those years I have seen exhilarating triumph, bitter tragedy, and everything in-between.

Herman Melville, the author of *Moby Dick*, observed "To produce a mighty book, you must choose a mighty theme." I can't think a theme mightier than your dreams. I believe truly and wholeheartedly in the power of books to change lives. To the college-bound, be imaginative!

Eric Bierker, January 2014

1-Avalanche University: Every Step Matters

It is not the mountain we conquer but ourselves.
Sir Edmund Hillary

The title of the February 2000 *Outside* magazine reads like a wind-weary tombstone:

"AND NONE CAME BACK"

Jerry Kanzler, Clare Pogreba, Ray Martin, Mark Levitan, and James Anderson, college students, in their late teens or early twenties. All of them were well-equipped expert mountain climbers with a spirit of adventure compelling them to be the first to ascend the north face of Mt. Cleveland in Glacier National Park in Montana, one of the United States' steepest vertical walls at over 4,000 feet.

That December 1969 these five were, in the words of author McKay Jenkins, who tells their compellingly tragic tale in his book, *The White Death*, "Mountaineering's best and brightest."[1]

Jenkins recounts that these young men had hiked Glacier National Park since they were toddlers. The mountains of Glacier National Park, particularly along the Continental Divide, where the watersheds that drain into the Pacific Ocean divide from those watersheds that drain into the Atlantic Ocean, get enormous amounts of snow --often more than 80 feet a winter--most of it falling on Mt. Cleveland. On December 26, confident and self-assured, the five boys set off despite the concerns of Park Ranger Bob Frauson's, who made note in his

7

station logbook: "Five boys checked out to climb Cleveland on a six-day expedition."

The boys never really had a chance. Jenkins writes, "Once a slab of snow becomes sufficiently unstable, it begins to slide downhill with almost unimaginable force...the average avalanche can generate 20 million horsepower, about 2,857 times that of an Amtrak locomotive. It was not until 6 months later, on June 29 after the spring had melted the snowpack that the boys' bodies were found roped together. The boys had not lived long enough to suffocate. They had been killed by the fall and carried a half mile down the slope, some 1500 vertical feet by a vast, tumbling, wall of snow. This was the biggest loss of life in any mountaineering expedition up until that time in the United States."

An avalanche is not unlike the danger facing many young adults, confident and self-assured, when they embark upon the journey to and through college. Every year I fret about my senior college-bound students entering this higher education avalanche zone.

In his May 2010 essay, *"The Third Rail Question on College?"* Scott Bittle writes: "A key point is the nation's college completion rate, with only 4 in 10 students graduating in four years. For some that's an argument that fewer people should be going to college--that those who drop out lack the commitment and academic qualifications to complete a college degree. When *Public Agenda* surveyed young people why they did or did not finish college, we found that those who dropped out said that the responsibilities became too much for them." [2]

Responsibilities such as mounting financial pressure, family problems, social conflict, lack of support, and academic difficulties, all conspire and combine to create a tragedy. Avalanche is an apt descriptor is it not?

The same avalanche that spells disaster on a mountain wreaks havoc on the lives of college-bound young people. Negative events and unwise choices cascade into a larger tragedy. This book has been written to help strengthen your footing and provide the direction for ~~you~~ *your* walk away from tragedy rather than into it.

Adolescence to Adulthood

The college transition is when the East of youth meets the West of adulthood with a significant change in psychological and physical geography. Climbing and crossing the Continental Divide of adolescence to adulthood is a time not only of great opportunity but also of great danger. The mountain can be viewed as an ideal metaphor for the college experience. Like the equipment that climbers use to anchor themselves to the rock, young people need a set of tools and strategies to make the difficult climb through the many challenges of the college transition process so that they can ultimately reach the summit.

Along this path avalanches and other dangers lurk. Yet, the *Mountain Climbing School/Santiam Alpine Club* notes that "Snow avalanche conditions for open slopes can often be predicted by monitoring the weather."[3] Good prediction and preparation creates the conditions for a strong and successful performance.

Just like mountain climbers, young adults must anticipate what their future college experiences will entail. The ultimate goal of college years is to become highly capable so that you can climb and conquer the mountains of life.

On the Edge: Transitioning Imaginatively to College is offered in the spirit of the following quote from Samuel Taylor Coleridge, "Advice is like snow: The softer it falls, the longer it dwells upon, and the deeper it sinks, into the mind."

When conveying the possibility for difficulty and danger it is critical to be specific and clear. To do otherwise does little to help. The avalanche idea is to rouse you to action. When the risks are downplayed and not explained in detail is it little wonder that students in the college transition often radically underestimate the challenges ahead?

There are those along the path who want to help, those who could care less, and probably some who may do you harm, either intentionally or unintentionally. You will be presented with both wonderful opportunities and serious challenges in college. Good choices over time are as steps in a journey to Commencement.

Heading to the Mountains

And why the mountain metaphor? Perhaps Edwin Bernbaum, Ph.D., who has designed and co-led the University of Pennsylvania Wharton Leadership Seminar treks to Mt. Everest in Nepal, describes it best. He writes in his essay *"Peak Paradigms: Mountain Metaphors of Leadership and Teamwork"*, "Mountains and mountain climbing provide some of our most dramatic and powerful metaphors for overcoming challenges. The summit of a peak is one of the clearest and most powerful symbols for attaining a goal or objective. The flexibility of mountain metaphors makes it easier to formulate win-win approaches to cooperative ventures. Although climbers can compete with each other or the mountain, they don't have to; everyone can get to the top and win without one side having to lose, as is a must in football or baseball. Climbing takes place not on an artificial, neatly controlled playing field but in the natural, mirroring the uncertainties of the real world."4 Uncertainties, like college.

The mountain is the grounds for success or failure but there is no limit to the number of victors. While proper preparation and a clear focus are essential, anyone can reach his or her peak potential. However, keep in mind that the mountain is also brutally unforgiving.

Around the time my wife Lina and I were out in Montana (Spanish for mountain) for a two-week adventure, a local neurosurgeon and expert climber Dr. William Labunetz tumbled to his death in Glacier National Park. Neurosurgeons are some of the world's most brilliant, highly-educated doctors. After earning a college degree (4-5 years), then graduating from medical school and completing an internship (4 years), the doctor enters a taxing neurosurgical residency program. A neurosurgical residency takes 5 to 7 years to complete. It is at 36 of age or so before a neurologist is out of school and fully prepared for the position. Not a person by training prone to be reckless, ill-informed, or rash.

Labunetz was climbing on the Iceberg Notch to Ahern Pass of the Ptarmigan Wall Traverse when he lost his footing and tragically his life. In a *Great Falls Tribune* story retired Great Falls Tribune Associate Editor Tom Kotynski wrote, "No one is sure exactly what caused Labunetz to fall but there is always risk involved, no matter how experienced a hiker may be."5 Kotynski continued in the newspaper article to say that the Ptarmigan Traverse is one of the premiere backcountry experiences in Glacier and a path that he "had no doubt Labunetz was capable of tackling."

Kotynski concludes, "The tragedy once again shows that caution and sound judgment must always be used when climbing in Glacier National Park." This intelligent well-trained man had all of the knowledge and skill to avoid tragedy. He took one wrong step and lost his life.

Don't think that similar tragedies can't or won't come your way. Though being prepared is an essential start, one must always remember that scaling "The Edge" is inherently a perilous journey. While not as stark as five adventuresome and extreme risk-taking young men perishing on Mt. Cleveland or a neurosurgeon tumbling 300 feet to his death, the college graduation rate in the United States is a catastrophe. What else can we call it?

What if there was an expedition to the top of a mountain in Glacier National Park, one where presumably--like those entering college--everyone going was qualified, and less than half made it in the allotted time to the top? What if there were avoidable dangers with even the majority of the hikers who made it to the apex? That fact should make you somewhat fearful.

Love Your Fear

A healthy fear about your future should motivate you to be serious about your life. The website www.fitnessandpower.com has a picture and these words about fear on its website:

I fear settling
Giving into the 'That is just the way it is" mindset
I fear dying without making my mark

I fear not feeling these fears anymore
And just floating along
These fears feed me, they nourish my drive
I love my fear

I have interacted with a lot of students in my days where a little more healthy fear would have been a good thing. I also have encountered many students who are so fearful of failing that they are nearly frozen and don't move forward and grow. Neither posture is correct. Some fear is essential, too much or not enough is bad. Walking the path to college has its share of vistas that both amaze and terrify. It should scare you to some degree that the choices that you make now, when you are a teenager, will help determine to a significant degree the direction of the rest of your life.

This is serious, you cannot afford to be complacent on your climb through college. Examine and reflect upon this chart from ACT illustrating the % of students getting to the mountaintop of graduation:

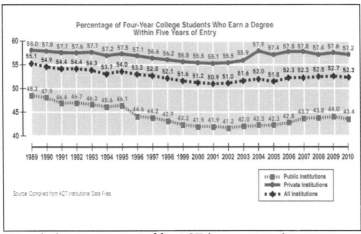

*Permission to use granted by ACT (www.act.org)

13

Around 50%? Pretty sobering statistic. Would you be eager to start the climb if it became clear upon reflection that you were not given the best maps, expertise, guidance, supplies, and equipment to be successful?

*A feature of this book will be a series of ideas for you to consider as you scale the mountain of college. These will be known as **EDGE IDEAS**, opportunities to reflect upon places in the journey, where a right or wrong step will be of great consequence.*

EDGE IDEA: Many going to college don't face their fears about the experience. Facing your fears is the first step of fixing your fears. What are your fears?

There is a term in mountaineering called *"Approach."* It is the section of the climb leading up to the most difficult section of the mountain. The senior year of high school is very similar to this Approach. If you are a high school senior you probably have already taken the SAT and/or ACT. You should be going through the process of applying to college or are waiting to hear back about whether you have been accepted at the college of your choice. These parts of the college preparation process are perhaps behind you. Possibly, you already know the college mountain that you are to climb.

As challenging as it has been up to this point, your greatest challenges lie ahead of you. My 25 years as an outreach counselor to college freshmen and as a high school counselor, as well as my college transition research in Educational Psychology, have shown me the dedication needed for success. The college transition is particularly critical. This first leg of the journey will often set the stage for the rest of your hike. A bad start more often than not leads to a bad end.

Looking back to reflect on your history is helpful in thinking about how your past will affect your future. The past will influence how you will respond to the challenge of college. Despite what you have experienced healthy or not don't let your past control your future. Understand your past but squarely face your future. Take it a day at a time and a step at a time.

Sir Edmund Hillary, the man who first stood atop Mt. Everest, summarized what he learned from a lifetime of high adventure and high danger climbing: "Don't look down." The past is down. The author Steven Covey writes, "Live out of your imagination, not your history."

One of my former students and I wrote back and forth on Facebook recently. She had a very damaging home life full of abuse and neglect. She had to put herself through college without any support, financial or otherwise, from home.

She just earned her Master's degree in France and she gave me permission to share the following message: "I guess, if one is to look on the bright side of everything that has happened to me, I have no attachments and no obligations to a family and so I can move about freely without feeling homesick or nostalgic. Moreover, I was fearless after I left my house, which I think is usually the opposite for most young students, and it opened a lot of doors for me." She was fearless in the right way.

Cory Booker, formerly the mayor of Newark, New Jersey, and now a U.S. Senator from New Jersey, issued this challenge to the graduating Class of 2012 in his Commencement speech at Stanford University, his Alma Mater: "In life you get one choice over and over again. That is to take conditions as they are or take responsibility for changing them." And change starts, as noted by Booker, from within. "Yesterday can be an anchor around your neck. Don't let past circumstance steal present opportunities."[6]

EDGE IDEA: The same energy that goes wasted into excuse-making is needed to overcome adversity.

It helps to be philosophical. The ancient Roman philosopher Boethius, writer of the book *The Consolation of Philosophy*, observed "Balance out the good things and the bad that have happened in your life and you will have to acknowledge that you are still way ahead. You are unhappy because you have lost those things in which you took pleasure? But you can also take comfort in the likelihood that what is now making you miserable will also pass away."

Hopefully, your parents, family, and other adults have provided you with a balance of high expectations and high support. If others have not set high expectations for you learn to set your own meaningful goals. Don't be too independent or too dependent. Climbing alone is not wise.

Here is a brief survey of what colleges offer as resources: Academic Advisement, Library Services, Campus Life (what clubs are on campus), Career Center, Counseling Center, Disability Services, Health Services, Public Safety, Peer Tutoring, Writing and Math Centers, Religious Life, Community Service, Greek Life, and Resident Life. Just like in high school, you have to want to be helped. Unlike high school, you must seek out opportunities. It is wise to ask for a hand.

There are of course radical differences between high school and college. Simply, college grants more freedom and more responsibility personally, academically, and socially. You are going to have to learn new climbing strategies for the extreme challenge. While high school challenged you to think in new ways, college life will force you to branch out and step out of your comfort zone into a wild environment. And yes, you are probably going to have to pay for at least some, if not most of it.

EDGE IDEA: You need inspiration not just information; that magical capacity to imagine great things and do great things.

Once the imaginative appetite is on high-burn then information is consumed voraciously like granola on the collegiate trail.

Failure & Falling Down

No matter how motivated, inspired, and hungry you are there is one simple fact of life: You are going to fail and even fall down sometimes. The trick is to brush yourself off and get back on your feet. Failure is a "feedback loop", it is not the end of the trail. You have to retrace your steps and get back on the right path. Have the courage to admit you are lost. It is rarely too late to start again.

Writer and Pastor Mark Batterson observes, "The cure for the fear of failure is not success. It's failure. The cure for the fear of rejection is not acceptance. It's rejection. You've got to be exposed to small quantities of whatever you are afraid of. That's how you build up immunity."[7]

17

Jeff Stibel writes, "I've said this before but it bears repeating: Success by failure is not an oxymoron. When you make a mistake, you're forced to look back and find out exactly where you went wrong, and formulate a new plan for your next attempt. By contrast, when you succeed, you don't always know exactly what you did right that made you successful."[8]

EDGE IDEA: Failure is a great teacher but only if you learn from it.

For those who don't learn the lesson, trouble tends to come first as a flake, then a snow drift, and then an avalanche. Know your resources and be aware of where and how to ask for help before you might need it. Don't take on too much too soon. Acclimate to the environment and get a sense for what is required before adding more activities and responsibilities beyond the essential.

Speaking of failure, one of the great storytellers of the past twenty years has a thing or two to say about the topic. In a Commencement address at Harvard, J.K. Rowling, author of the *Harry Potter* series, said, "So why do I talk about the benefits of failure? Simply because failure meant a stripping away of the inessential. I stopped pretending to myself that I was anything other than what I was, and began to direct all my energy into finishing the only work that mattered to me. Had I really succeeded at anything else, I might never have found the determination to succeed in the one arena I believed I truly belonged. I was set free, because my greatest fear had been realized, and I was still alive, and I still had a daughter whom I adored, and I had an old typewriter and a big idea.

Rock bottom became the solid foundation on which I rebuilt my life." She added, "You might never fail on the scale I did, but some failure in life is inevitable. It is impossible to live without failing at something, unless you live so cautiously that you might as well not have lived at all--in which case, you fail by default."[9]

College failure? Hey, it's going to happen. You might occasionally fail a test; you'll have relationship conflict; you will struggle to find your identity. College, like anything worthwhile, is difficult.

EDGE IDEA: Observe successful students and learn from them. You may have to customize the tools and techniques to fit your unique personality and conditions but you don't usually have to invent such tools and techniques.

Avoiding 200K Debt Mountain

Kelli Space in her essay *"I Went to College and All I Got Was This $ 200,000 Bill"* writes, "Looking back, I always wonder what was going through my mind throughout college, as I was just chugging along and accumulating all that debt. Sure I thought about it; sometimes I cried and phoned home for something to assuage my anxiety, but still I stayed at Northeastern (a university in Boston). I know the fact that I was the first to attend college in my family played a role, as did the idea that the best school that offered you admission was the one you would attend, no questions asked."

"These were obviously misconceptions that I had to learn the hard way, as clearly no one else was going to correct me along the way."[10] Kelli obviously succeeded in graduating from college but she did not correctly think through the costs of her lack of preparation in paying for it--and she is now paying for it with interest.

In college expenses, aim for quality and economy. College students must be clear-minded about the prospects of success balanced with the accumulation of debt. Some borrowing to pay for college can be a good investment but you must carefully weigh the risks of doing so. If you are entering a career that does not pay particularly well you had better know that ahead of time. It is possible to live frugally and still have a wonderfully fulfilling life but if the bills keep coming and you have no money it will be extremely stressful. That is a mountain you don't want to get stuck on when the cold and bitter winds of unpaid bills howl. Save money when/where you can--books, lap top, food, etc. The best you can afford at the lowest price.

EDGE IDEA: Always examine and test your gear, your assumptions and ideas about college.

Finish, Not Just Go, To College

At the 1968 Olympics in Mexico City, in the men's marathon event, the last person to finish was a bloodied and bandaged Tanzanian named John Akhwari. While competing he fell badly cutting his knee and dislocating the joint. He kept running, ending last among the 57 competitors who finished the race (74 had started).

www.youtube.com/watch?v=Hq3rOMnLGBk

The Gold winner of the marathon Mamo Wolde of Ethiopia, finished with a time of 2:20:26. Akhwari finished in 3:25:27 when there were only a few thousand people left in the stadium and the sun had gone down.

When asked why he had continued on in such pain, Akhwari said: "My country did not send me 7,000 miles to start the race. They sent me 7,000 miles to finish."

I have worked with far too many students who think that GETTING TO COLLEGE is the goal. WRONG, WRONG, WRONG. The goal is to GRADUATE FROM COLLEGE.

Junko Tabei, after becoming first woman to climb Mt. Everest, said "Technique and ability alone do not get you to the top; it is willpower that is the most important. This willpower you cannot buy with money or be given by others...it rises from your heart."[11] *GUTS !!!*

2 - Get Climbing!

You cannot climb a mountain if you will not risk a fall.
Rick Beneteau

Over one million acres straddling the Continental Divide, Glacier National Park in Northwest Montana is among the wildest land in the lower 48 United States. There are 26 active glaciers, 200 lakes, and one hundred and fifty named mountains. Mt. Cleveland, the highest at 10,500 feet, rises steeply above the terrain. First scaled in 1920 it is also the mountain that claimed the lives of the five boys. Pristine wilderness, protected from 20th and 21st century commercial development, these mountains are sacred to the Blackfeet Native Americans.

The settings of the stories in this book are in or near Glacier National Park where my wife and I journeyed in September 2009, including a trip to Missoula, the college-town where the University of Montana is located. We visited Montana while I was in the midst of writing my dissertation on *College Preparation Knowledge*. The mountains and the stories I will share are powerful metaphors for the college experience.

Close to two million visitors explore Glacier National Park yearly. The main road through the park is the Going-to-the-Sun Road that travels 53 miles throughout the park's interior. According to the website www.hikinginglacier.com, the road that crosses the Continental Divide via Logan's Pass can accumulate up to 80 feet of snow in the winter. It typically takes two and a half months to plow the road free of snow for the visiting tourists in the summer who usually visit after Memorial Day and before

Labor Day. In Glacier National Park there is only a limited seasonal window each year to cross.

EDGE IDEA: Late adolescence and early adulthood is the best time of life to create independence, establish firm beliefs, and to graduate from college.

It does not mean that you cannot go to college later when you are an adult but getting to college graduation will never be less burdened by other demands and responsibilities than when you are a young adult. If you are not ready it is better to wait. Yet, be careful about frittering away precious time.

There is really no definitive answer whether those five young men--Jerry Kanzler, Clare Pogreba, Ray Martin, Mark Levitan, and James Anderson--were just being plain reckless in trying to climb Mt. Cleveland when they did or if it was an extreme adventure gone tragically wrong. The best thing tragedies can do is to teach powerful and painful lessons. It is true, as T.S. Eliot wrote, "Only those who will risk going too far can possibly find out how far one can go." No risk equals no reward.

Pastor Mark Batterson shared this in his sermon *"Looking Foolish"* on December 20, 2006:

"A few months ago I was reading the writings of John Muir--the founder of the Sierra Club. Muir is tough to describe but the love of nature was the central passion of his life. He spent his life studying it, protecting it, and appreciating it. One of my favorite Muir moments happened in December of 1874. John Muir was staying with a friend at his cabin in the Sierra Mountains and a winter storm set in. The wind was so strong that it bent the trees over backwards. But instead of retreating to the safety of the cabin, Muir chased the storm! He found a mountain ridge, climbed to the top of a giant Douglas Fir tree, and held on for dear life for several hours feasting his senses on the sights and sounds and scents. John Muir was no stranger to danger. He climbed mountains and crossed rivers and explored glaciers. But there is something about this mental picture of John Muir climbing a one-hundred foot Douglas fir tree during a storm that is iconic." As cited by Batterson, Muir wrote this in his journal about the experience:

> *"When the storm began to sound*
> *I lost no time in pushing out into*
> *the woods to enjoy it. For on such*
> *occasions, Nature always has*
> *something rare to show us, and*
> *the danger to life and limb is*
> *hardly greater than one would*
> *experience crouching deprecatingly*
> *beneath a roof."*

Batterson concludes, in the words of writer Eugene Peterson:

> *"The story of John Muir climbing to*
> *the top of that storm-whipped Douglas Fir*
> *is a standing rebuke against*
> *becoming a mere spectator to life."*[12]

Author John Green asks, "What is the point of being alive is you don't at least try to do something remarkable?"Despite the real risks of going to college, the rewards are indisputable. College graduates statistically will earn a million more dollars in a lifetime, have much lower rates of unemployment, and have significantly greater health, happiness, broader social networks, and more advanced intellectual skills, than those with just a high school diploma.[13]

EDGE IDEA: There are no promises, only probabilities, yet college creates better chances of leading a successful, purposeful life.

The I-PASS Model of College Transition(© *Eric Bierker*)

So, how can you process the college transition and commence in climbing the mountain?

If you want to make the transition to the college mountain more effective and less overwhelming, it is helpful to view it as a Personal, Academic, and Social Scene transition. Doing so gives you a 3-dimensional perspective and assists you to identify the steps necessary to get to the apex.

This transition involves you (the Personal), your intellectual task of ascending through the course-work and earning credits in completing the requirements for a degree (the Academic), and experiencing first-hand the environment of the mountain itself--its diversity of life and its innate characteristics (the Social Scene).

Personal – This is what you bring with you to college in all of its complexity (aptitudes, interests, values, habits, personality, and past) and what your beliefs are and will be. Identity issues of who am I?; What do I believe?; What is my purpose in life?; are the existential and often philosophical questions that students ask themselves during this time. College has a way of drawing such questions to the surface because you know that you now have adult-like responsibilities and are no longer a child. Life becomes more serious and so do your questions.

25

Academic – This is where you grasp that the intellectual climb on the college path is more difficult, complex, and stimulating than high school. Or at least should be. It is possible to avoid rigor but you do so to the detriment of your own development. You will often wonder more about "What does this mean to me and my life?" when learning material and information.

Your academic experiences will interact with both your personal identity and your social culture empowering you to see and understand connections among all three aspects, thus creating a Worldview. What the Germans call *Weltanschauung*, a way to view the world.

There will also be more dangers of getting lost. Ultimately college is about learning about a specific academic discipline and also developing a perspective on how your knowledge relates to other disciplines and then applying it to your day-to-day professional and personal life in one way or another. Majoring in something means that you need to select a path, for you cannot walk in twelve directions at once and make any progress. But you can change your path if need be.

Social Scene – You will have the opportunity to develop diverse relationships, informal to intimate, in the unique once-in-a lifetime social context of college. Many of your peers and professors may be from different communities, cultures, and even countries from you. College provides the truly awesome opportunity to potentially choose among thousands of these people to be friends with. But you really can't actually be friends with 5000 people despite what Facebook permits. Pick your 20-25 closest friends carefully. They will influence you for good or for ill more than anything else. You can have many more acquaintances in college than 20-25 individuals just not more than 20-25 friends.

Out of those friends, you will have a tighter group of 5 to 7 really close friends. You are going to have to make weighty decisions without a whole lot of outside and external guidance besides your peer group. Choose your friends wisely. It is difficult to change others' minds to see things the way you do. Reserve the closest ring in your social circle for those who already share the same values and destination. This is particularly true of any potential romantic relationship.

No two colleges are the same academically or socially. There is a complex interaction between the individual and the environment that is unique to your identity, experiences, and life journey. For instance, you might decide to go to an elite liberal arts college that is Mt. Everest-like in regards to that institution's academic and intellectual demands and expectations. You will have a much different experience there as compared to attending the local mid-sized mountain of a state university where it is less competitive. You must invest a serious and substantial amount of time and effort to determine which college campus to call home for some of the most important years of your life. You have to find the college that is right for you.

The Qualities of Transitioning Well

The National Resource Center at the University of South Carolina (www.sc.edu/fye) documents university orientation programs assisting freshmen with the college transition. Such programs demonstrate a common curriculum and stated objectives, with only minor differences.

The skills these programs seek to impart are:

To think critically and make wise decisions.

To manage time effectively.

To be mature, civil, and responsible.

To be healthy in body and mind as to achieve one's potential.

To be familiar with the campus and the services offered.

To develop supportive relationships with professors and peers, as well as other individuals in the campus environment and off-campus.

EDGE IDEA: The higher you aspire personally, academically, and socially, the harder it is going to be. You will derive enormous satisfaction from doing hard things and overcoming them.

Difficulties and obstacles that many college students will encounter are family problems, homesickness, time-management, studying, money, part-time employment, depression, health issues, friend and roommate conflicts, alcohol/partying, romantic relationships, choosing a major, and career indecision.

One thing is certain. The college transition requires an equal balance of preparation in a number of different areas, Personal, Academic, and Social.

Shangri-La U: A Campus Called Perfection?

Shangri-La is an alluring fictional place described in the 1933 novel *Lost Horizon*[14] by British author James Hilton. In the book, Shangri-La is a mystical, harmonious valley, gently guided from a lamasery (a monastery for the monks known as lamas) enclosed in the western end of the Kunlun Mountains. As a result of the book, Shangri-La has become synonymous with any earthly paradise, but particularly a mythical Himalayan utopia--a permanently happy land, isolated from the outside world. In *Lost Horizon* the people who live in Shangri-La are almost immortal, living years beyond the normal lifespan and only very slowly aging in appearance.

A senior proclaimed to me a few years ago that the Ivy League university she was accepted to and planning to attend was "perfect" as if it were some sort of Shangri-La.

Although I did think that the college was a great fit for her I specifically counseled her that "it is not perfect." She might have an obnoxious roommate with B.O.; perhaps she would have a professor or two or three who'd be quite pompous and uninspiring, and experience other less-than-ideal realities that would prove to her that her college was not perfect.

There is no SLU, Shangri-La University. Again, every year, I have to remind a good number of my college-bound seniors that their college of choice is not ideal. I want to inoculate them against unreasonable expectations.

EDGE IDEA: Perfection is never possible. Disenchantment and dissatisfaction inevitably follow perfectionism.

29

One of the first burdens in the college transition process you need to jettison is the weight that comes with expecting "perfection."

Personally - An attitude of thinking that the perfect is even possible.

Academically – That all your learning will be peak experiences and not sheer drudgery at times.

Socially – Expecting your relationships to bring mostly pleasure and not also a good measure of pain.

Most colleges look great from a distance. Let me illustrate. While in Montana, I biked to the top of Big Mountain (6817 feet in elevation) and gazed upon the beautiful and pristine Lake Whitefish below. I walked down to the beach of Lake Whitefish later in the day and went for a swim. It had been many years since I have been in a lake so clear. It was what it looked like at a distance. Many lakes and rivers are not.

College recruitment posters, websites, and other media, depict their school as a Shangri-La U., showing happy and smiling collegians, a clear and sparkling campus as beautiful as Lake Whitefish near Glacier National Park. There is often a decidedly multi-ethnic vibe in the media where the White, Latino, Asian, and African-American students look like the best of chums ready for a group hug and some ice cream after the picturesque photo shoot on campus--and it is never raining. Yet, when you get there, that ideal is not the reality you experience. At some point you'll be swimming in the water daily for at least four years. You need to find a good, not perfect, fit.

EDGE IDEA: Your college choice is a combination of using your head (facts) and following your heart (intuition). Don't lean too far to either the head or heart side.

3 – The Academic Ascent

A little Learning is a dang'rous Thing;
Drink deep, or taste not the Pierian Spring:
There shallow Draughts intoxicate the Brain,
And drinking largely sobers us again.
Alexander Pope

Your Brain on Fire

We never know when real authentic learning might take place. One of my most powerful learning experiences in Montana came not in a cavernous lecture hall but at a picnic table in East Glacier, Montana. The professor? A Polish man named Bart. A cook at the Whistle Stop Café. And here is the amazing story he shared.

It had been a sunny day in a small Polish village before the outbreak of World War II. In lightning-like strikes German planes ominously strafed the blue skies and the townspeople scattered for their lives as the massive bombs hit the ground and exploded into deadly fragments.

The attack came without any advance warning or declaration of war. Buildings were flattened and fires burned the wreckage and rubble to ashes. People and horses were dismembered. Imagine the mayhem, the destruction, the sounds and the smells. Chaos and destruction had come quickly and the loss of life and property was immediate and apocalyptic.

After the planes exited the skies above, and as the smoke started to clear on the ground, it was discovered that a baby girl in a cart on the street had somehow survived while everyone and everything around her had been destroyed. She had miraculously lived through the bombing without even a scratch. It was Bart's mom who was the baby girl in the cart.

Seated at a picnic table in the early afternoon sun while a tranquil breeze blew, a day probably not so much different than the day of the bombing, Bart imparted his story. I paid rapt attention. There was no test at the end or term paper to write or speech that I had to give. Nonetheless, I was riveted.

I have learned a lot of facts about World War II in classrooms in my days as a student ...which countries fought and why, how long it lasted, what the names of the major actors were and what they did. Yet, never had I come so close to the actual events as I did that day in East Glacier seventy years later. I entered into his story and life narrative not abstractly but personally.

Norman Podhoretz, in his essay in the book *My Columbia: Reminiscences of University Life*, notes of his years as an undergraduate at Columbia University, "I thought history was a series of past events...I did not know that I was a product of a tradition, that past ages had been inhabited by men and women like myself, and the things that they had done bore a direct relation to me and the world in which I lived....it set my brain on fire." [15]

I say "Amen!" to what Danielle LaPorte asks in her book *The Firestarter Sessions*:

Would you rather be sufficient or masterful?

Would you rather be bright or a freaking supernova?

Would you rather be well-rounded or on your own leading edge?[16]

The band Listener has lyrics in their song *"Most Roads Lead to Home"* that radiates this message:

"Look at the sound of all these people on fire
I want to be on fire
Do you want to be on fire?
But we don't love ourselves enough
We pack our hearts with medicine
And choke our lungs with broke down tries of lesser
men."

EDGE IDEA: It is with an incandescent attitude that you must enter all the potential learning experiences in your life. Don't settle for the smoldering ashes of mediocrity, burn on fire.

The academic ascent will cost you if you truly want to develop expertise. Like a fire burning, it will make you gasp for oxygen and consume you. If it doesn't you should wonder if you are really learning much of anything.

Yes, there is a time when you need to call it a day but remember your zone of performance can be measurably expanded by effort where you perform at a higher level in the future because of the energy you expended today. Martial Arts legend Bruce Lee said this quite well, "If you always put limits on everything you do, physical or anything else, it will spread into your work and into your life. There are no limits. There are only plateaus, and you must not stay there, you must go beyond them."

Take those professors, read those books, and attend those talks from outside speakers, who share the luminosity of their academic discipline.

In the Harvard Commencement address mentioned previously, J.K. Rowling went on to discuss imagination. She noted that when she was unemployed she volunteered at Amnesty International on behalf of persecuted people in totalitarian regimes.

"Now you might think that I chose my second theme, the importance of imagination, because of the part it played in rebuilding my life, but that is not wholly so. Though I personally will defend the value of bedtime stories to my last gasp, I have learned to value imagination in a much broader sense. Imagination is not only the uniquely human capacity to envision that which is not, and therefore the fount of all invention and innovation. In its arguably most transformative and revelatory capacity, it is the power that enables us to empathize with humans whose experiences we have never shared.

Amnesty mobilizes thousands of people who have never been tortured or imprisoned for their beliefs to act on behalf of those who have. The power of human empathy, leading to collective action, saves lives, and frees prisoners. Ordinary people, whose personal well-being and security are assured, join together in huge numbers to save people they do not know, and will never meet. My small participation in that process was one of the most humbling and inspiring experiences of my life.

Unlike any other creature on this planet, humans can learn and understand, without having experienced. They can think themselves into other people's places. Of course, this is a power, like my brand of fictional magic that is morally neutral. One might use such an ability to manipulate, or control, just as much as to understand or sympathize.

And many prefer not to exercise their imaginations at all. They choose to remain comfortably within the bounds of their own experience, never troubling to wonder how it would feel to have been born other than they are. They can refuse to hear screams or to peer inside cages; they can close their minds and hearts to any suffering that does not touch them personally; they can refuse to know.

I might be tempted to envy people who can live that way, except that I do not think they have any fewer nightmares than I do.

Choosing to live in narrow spaces leads to a form of mental agoraphobia, and that brings its own terrors. I think the willfully unimaginative see more monsters. They are often more afraid.

What is more, those who choose not to empathize enable real monsters. For without ever committing an act of outright evil ourselves, we collude with it, through our own apathy. One of the many things I learned at the end of that Classics corridor down which I ventured at the age of 18, in search of something I could not then define, was this, written by the Greek author Plutarch: *"What we achieve inwardly will change outer reality."*

That is an astonishing statement and yet proven a thousand times every day of our lives. It expresses, in part, our inescapable connection with the outside world, the fact that we touch other people's lives simply by existing."[17]

The Purpose of Education: Knowing, Not Knowing

In Greek mythology, the Macedonia Pierian Spring mentioned in the Pope poem at the beginning of this chapter was sacred to the Muses[18]. The Pierian

Spring was located on Mt. Olympus, the home of the 12 Olympian gods of the ancient Greek world and the highest peak in Greece. As the metaphorical source of knowledge of art and science it was popularized by this line in Alexander Pope's poem.

Drink a little of the spring of knowledge, get big-headed. Drink a lot, you may sober up and become wise. Learning should make us humble not haughty. For it is through this genuine learning that we grow as human beings. More than mere intelligence, it is wisdom.

Tim Dalrymple, managing editor of *Evangelical Portal,* explains this idea in his essay *"An Open Letter to a College Freshman."* He writes, "Intelligence is cheap, because it's inherited freely; wisdom is of inestimable value because it's gained through suffering and sacrifice and years of hard study and experience. Every night at Stanford I watched the most intelligent people doing the most foolish of deeds, chasing after the most worthless of goals, and believing the most baseless of things. Their intelligence did nothing to make them more loving or joyful or genuine.

In fact, in many cases it led them astray, as they came to worship their own intellectual powers along with the admiration and accolades and material consolations they could win. They became immune to criticism, self-indulgent, and chasers of intellectual fashions. When you love the reputation of intelligence, then you will do and believe those things that will sustain that reputation. Intelligence does not make you more likely to do what is right or believe what is true."[19]

Knowledge, like and endless mountain, is massive and we can never master it even as we climb and conquer. People get in trouble when they think they know more than they do. In *The White Death: Tragedy and Heroism in an Avalanche Zone* book, McKay Jenkins shares a quote from a man named DeSanto who was very familiar with Glacier National Park after spending 21 years there as a Park Ranger: "The best thing wilderness experiences can teach you is humility. The fact is the more experience you have, the more you realize you don't have all of the answers."

Jenkins reflects: "DeSanto's sentiments, of course, apply broadly in the backcountry, as perhaps they do to life generally; only the foolish can convince themselves that they know everything, or even can know everything. Life, for those willing to learn, has a way of teaching the value of not knowing--bowing respectfully before forces more powerful or mysterious than might be imagined."

Becoming educated does not mean that you corner the Universe for answers; it is more that you have an awareness of the vastness of knowledge and a curiosity to intellectually explore the unknown.

Going to college is not just about securing employment in a chosen field, it is also for inculcating a love for learning and developing the academic and intellectual tools to make such an exploration possible.

EDGE IDEA: Knowing that you don't know is true knowledge.

Don't be complicit when someone from whom you are trying to learn lowers the challenge and reduces the rigor. It is only you who loses in the end. Further, don't be content with an inferior education because of your own choices and subpar performance.

You might be concerned about the environment, world health, technology, politics, culture, art.

Get informed, get educated, and engage. Most professors are more than eager to assist you in your learning if you just show that you care. Ultimately, you set your own standards and create the challenge that you must overcome. In order to reach greatness you must continue striving to ascend taller peaks.

Your classroom experiences should be as a path to breathtaking academic and intellectual vistas. Some of those vistas might include spending a semester abroad or at sea, getting to know people outside of your cultural or ethnic group on campus as a way of challenging your internal intellectual presuppositions and expanding your cultural awareness, and taking the harder course where you will actually learn a lot even though your grade might be lower as a consequence. If you want to spend thousands of dollars just goofing around on the mountain, you have squandered your time and money.

Getting Organized GPS: Getting from Here to There

It is absolutely fundamental that you develop a system to handle the demands of the collegiate experience. Being disorganized is dangerous and your high school experience may have not required you to internalize time management principles. Your parents, teachers, and school counselor may have created a lot of safety nets and second chances for you with incessant reminders and the like. I see far too many bright teenagers use the support system in high school as an excuse to coast and slack off. Then, when such students arrive on the college campus, many of them have not developed the habits, conditioning, and skills necessary for the challenges ahead of them.

Losing whatever momentum they could have developed in high school, they now have to start from zero. (You make habits, habits then make you.)

EDGE IDEA: Being organized is prioritizing your energy and effort intelligently.

Good for you if you have avoided this cliff. You are way ahead already. Your schedule in college is your essential map. It pays great dividends to study the terrain. Here is a sample route:

	MON	TUE	WED	THU	FRI	SAT	SUN
7-8	------7:45----	------7:45--	DRESS & BREAKFAST	--7:45----	------7:45-----		
8-9	DRILL	DRILL	DRESS & BREAKFAST	DRILL	DRILL	DRESS & BREAKFAST	
9-10	SPANISH 2	SPANISH 2	SPANISH 2 X-HOUR	SPANISH 2	SPANISH 2		DRESS & BREAKFAST
10-11	CHEM 6	PSYCH 6	CHEM 6	PSYCH 6	CHEM 6		
11-12	------11:15------		------11:15------		------11:15------		
12-1	------12:30------		------12:30------	CHEM 6 X-HOUR	------12:30------		
1-2	------1:45----		------1:45----	LUNCH	------1:45---		
2-3							
3-4		CHEM 6 LAB	PSYCH 6 X-HOUR				
4-5	PHYS. ED.		PHYS. ED.				
5-6							
6-7				DINNER			
7-8							CHEM 6 STUDY GROUP
8-9							
9-10							
10-11							
11-12			SLEEP				

* Permission to use template granted by Dartmouth College

It is crucial that you create a visual representation of scheduled times/commitments which are consistent week-to-week and will not change. Use iCloud or some program like it. Only then can you figure out when you have time for everything else.

How much time do you have in a day? How about a week? A month? A semester? The correct answer is "the same as everyone else." Thus, how you use your "free" time often becomes one of the key strategies you as a student can utilize to make the most of your climb, what to do when. Here is a quick breakdown on where time goes in college per week:

Total Time Available = 168 hours (24 X 7)

Sleep = 49 hours (7 hours a night)

Eating = 10 hours (1.5 hours a day)

Showering and Dressing = 7 hours (1 hour a day)

Classes = 20 hours (5 classes X 3 hours a week plus to/from class)

Studying = 30 hours (often more but this is minimum)

Exercise = 3 hours (lifting, aerobic, stretching)

Remaining Time Available = 49 hours a week!

How you use these 49 hours makes all of the difference between success and failure, presuming that you pay attention in class. You only have so much time and prioritizing it well is your most important responsibility.

In my years as an Outreach Counselor to college freshmen, what made most of the difference between success and failure of my students was how they used their time. The successful students were those who used their time wisely versus those who wasted it. The wasting of time was not generally getting drunk, smoking weed, and/or sleeping around. It was playing pool, watching TV, hanging out, video games, and sleeping. Then, the avalanche buried them. Small decisions day-by-day determined destiny.

Free time can have high costs. For example if you engage in riotous behavior in your "free time" odds are it is going to carry over into your non-free time. <u>Put in your calendar the steps to complete a task, not just due dates of tests, term papers, and projects.</u> You must track your tasks and manage your time effectively to ensure that you are making progress like markers on a trail. After you have blocked out the times that you are not available, then plan your remaining activities, including your social life. It is also very important to see your semester as a whole in terms of big events and deadlines.

DARTMOUTH COLLEGE SPRING TERM 2011 AT A GLANCE

Month	Sunday	Monday	Tuesday	Wednesday	Thursday	Friday	Saturday
March	27 Online check-in begins	28 Spring term classes begin/ Publication of Prospectus of Courses for period 11X-13S	29	30 Online check-in ends at 4pm	31	1 Deadline for spring term prospective graduates in residence to elect/change a major or minor	2
April	3	4 Deadline for return of degree applications by prospective June graduates who were not in residence in the Winter	5	6 Final day for sophomores to file major cards and revised enrollment pattern requests	7	8 Final day to establish official and final two-, three-, or four-course load	9
	10	11	12 Final day to NRO a course	13	14	15 Final day for first-year students to submit enrollment patterns	16
	17	18	19	20	21	22	23 Course Timetable available for summer term
	24	25	26	27	28 First day of Summer term course election	29	30

* Permission to use template granted by Dartmouth College

There are times in the semester where you will be extremely busy so advanced preparation and planning is needed. Smart phones with calendar functions provide the powerful tools and technology to get organized, so use them.

EDGE IDEA: Every minute matters. Make the most of each moment, particularly in the college environment where you will be granted more distracting social opportunities than any other time in your life.

Final Thoughts About Time From Mr. Rogers

"You rarely have time for everything you want in this life, so you need to make choices. And hopefully your choices can come from a deep sense of who you are...Some days, doing the best we can do may still fall short of what we would like to be able to do, but life isn't perfect on any front, and doing what we can with what we have is the most we should expect of ourselves or anyone else."[20]

Fred Rogers, American educator, Presbyterian minister, songwriter, and television host (March 20, 1928 – February 27, 2003).

4 – The Calling of the Mountains

There is something in man which responds to the challenge of this mountain and goes out to meet it, that the struggle is the struggle of life itself upward and forever upward. What we get from this adventure is just sheer joy.
Sir George Mallory

Pointless?

On an unusually balmy, placid September afternoon at the University of Montana, with students riding bikes, playing Frisbee, and hanging out on the Quad, my wife and I visited an exhibition of Pulitzer Prize winning photographs.

A photograph of an emaciated Sudanese child with a vulture perched a foot or two away waiting for the child to die had shocked the world and brought great admiration and harsh condemnation for the photographer of that picture.

This is the tragic story of South African photographer Kevin Carter. His story raises a difficult and profound question: What is success in this world? A career where you receive adulation and applause as being one of the best at what you do--fame and fortune? Kevin Carter had it all. It wasn't enough.

Kevin Carter was a photojournalist who had cut his teeth as a photographer covering the violence in South Africa under Apartheid. He developed a reputation, with some other South African photographers called *"The Bang-Bang Club,"* as an individual who would go into highly volatile and violent situations to take pictures, often putting himself in enormous risk of harm.

On assignment to the Sudan to photograph the famine in 1993, Carter took a picture of the starving and emaciated girl who was about 4 years old. She was sitting on the ground, clearly having exhausted all her energy while trying to get to a food line. As mentioned, accompanying this girl in the photograph was a vulture perched nearby waiting for her to die so it could eat her corpse. It's an incredibly moving photo that instills compassion and deep disturbance, all at the same time.

See this link for the photograph and more details on this scene and about Carter's life in general: www.flatrock.org.nz/topics/odds_and_oddities/ultimate_in_unfair.htm

When the *New York Times* published the photograph on March 26, 1993, it shocked the world. Soon thereafter, Carter garnered praise for his photograph, as well as an enormous amount of criticism, for not doing more to help the girl get to the food station. Warned by authorities to not touch the starving children because of diseases, Carter took the picture, chased away the vulture, and left the girl there, presumably for dead, then wept by a tree for a long time. Ultimately, the picture galvanized world action to provide aid.

On May 14, 1994, Carter won the top honor for a photographer in the world--the Pulitzer Prize, in New York City. He was seemingly on top of his profession and the world itself. The prize both intensified the acclaim and the animosity of others. The psychological toll of taking tragic photographs, and problems in his personal life, made his own life's photograph darker and darker.

A few weeks before winning the Pulitzer Prize, one of his close photographer buddies whom he had worked with throughout his professional career in such hellish situations had been shot and killed leaving a wife and children behind. Carter was deeply troubled by this, feeling he should have been the one to take the bullet.

There were suspicions that Carter was also getting more heavily into drugs and alcohol, and trying to deal with his demons through addictive and self-destructive behaviors. On Wednesday, July 27, 1994, Kevin Carter committed suicide by inhaling carbon monoxide from the fumes of his pick-up truck next to a small river in Johannesburg, South Africa where he used to play as a child.

In his suicide note, he wrote "The pain of life overrides the joy to the point that joy does not exist anymore." His photo saved tens of thousands of lives. Somehow he lost sight of his passion in the midst of his pain and his life became pointless.

Finding the Point

What about you? What captures your imagination and interest? What pursuit do you do, where minutes become hours and it seems like just a moment? Time flies, the tasks are invigorating, the effort, despite being difficult at times, is fun and creates exhilaration and joy. That is a big clue for what you are to pursue vocationally. Perhaps you know the true story of the homeless man Chris Garner, who went on to become a highly successful stockbroker, whose life was played by Will Smith in the film *Pursuit of Happyness*? Carmine Gallo, in his *Forbes* essay *"Homeless Man Turned Millionaire Offers the Best Advice I Ever Got"*, writes the following: "I knew the Oakland, California, subway station Gardner had slept in because I passed it every day on my train trip into San Francisco. I had plenty of time to contemplate the advice he gave, words that changed the course of my career.

"How did you find the strength, the spirit, to keep going?" I asked Gardner. *"Carmine, here's the secret to success: Find something you love to do so much, you can't wait for the sun to rise to do it all over again."*[21]

I have a former student who wanted to be a rock-and-roll radio station deejay. He hung around the station, did sandwich runs for the staff, learned the ropes for two long years, and then got his break when the station could not find a deejay one night in an emergency. He stepped up to the mike. Ironically, his name was Mike. Soon, he had the 4-midnight shift. He paid his dues until a door opened and he walked through it. Sylvester Stallone said, "Dreams cost nothing. They are free. The hard part is keeping them going."How can you get paid to do what you already love to do? There are steps that you need to take to discover and fulfill your passion. You may have to have another job to support your dream so that you can pay the rent, put a roof over your head, and food on the table. Over time, you could get to a place where you are making money and finding meaning. Or maybe you won't get paid in dollars but in something else you value. Don't make money your only goal. There are many miserable people with more money than they could spend in 1,000 years.

EDGE IDEA: Your dream will cost you more than you think. Much more. Still, it is worth it.

Crucial Skill for the 21ˢᵗ Century Climb? Creativity

As your generation faces the reality of downsized opportunity, the predominant qualities you have to nurture are your imagination and creativity. You can't follow the well-traveled paths to where you want to be; you are going to have to blaze your own trail. You can have fellow-travelers yet retain your uniqueness. Develop your character so that you are indispensible. In an online *Inc. Magazine* article titled *"10 Tips on Hiring for Creativity"*[22] Tim Donnelly interviewed executives from cutting edge firms about the attributes they look for in new hires:

Strategic thinkers who can go from an idea to end goals within an established timeframe.

Who have technical skill.

Who communicate effectively.

Those who know a lot about a little and a little about a lot. Called "T" people. Broad and Deep.

Are creative at bringing differing ideas together to form something new.

Who are curious and willing to learn new things.

Who work well independently as well as collaboratively.

Thrive off of open-ended challenges where the answers are not obvious.

Who are flexible.

Those who are humble, authentic, and honest.

You will notice that the skills prospective employees are after go far beyond the information you will learn inside of classroom. To develop these necessary skills you will need to break out of the safe four walls and seek out opportunities in the wild world of unpredictability. Seth Godin, in the book *Tribes*, writes, "Life is too short to fight the forces of change. Life's too short to do what you hate all day...The marketplace rewards innovation: Things that are fresh, stylish, remarkable, and new. Interesting side effect: Creating products and services that are remarkable is fun. Doing work that's fun is engaging. So not surprisingly, making things that are successful is a great way to spend your time."[23] Apple, one of the world's most successful companies, was started by two Steves in a garage in the mid-1970's in California. Since then, it has conquered the peak of the corporate world through extreme creativity and relentless innovation.

One of the founders, the late Steve Jobs, said: "Creativity is just connecting things. When you ask creative people how they did something, they feel a little guilty because they didn't really do it, they just saw something. It seemed obvious to them after a while. That's because they were able to connect experiences they've had and synthesize new things. And the reason they were able to do that was that they've had more experiences or they have thought more about their experiences than other people. Unfortunately, that's too rare a commodity. A lot of people in our industry (technology) haven't had very diverse experiences. So they don't have enough dots to connect, and they end up with very linear solutions without a broad perspective on the problem. The broader one's understanding of the human experience, the better design we will have."[24] Walter

Isaacson, Steve Jobs' biographer, told the magazine *Fast Company* "His whole life was a combination of mystical enlightenment thinking with hardcore rational thought...He had an intuition for connecting artistry with technology and that allows you to make imaginative leaps."[25] Jobs leveraged a combination of the humanities and sciences to fold highly sophisticated products into intensely simple designs.

"The Macintosh turned out so well because the people working on it were musicians, artists, poets and historians--who also happened to be excellent computer scientists,"[26] Jobs once told the *New York Times*. It is not either science or art; it is both. Know your field as comprehensively as possible but also take the time to think about areas outside of your expertise, and how your knowledge relates to that arena of knowledge. When you start to see those connections then you are beginning to think imaginatively.

Ponder this advice from Ira Glass, the host and producer of the Public Radio/Television show *This American Life:* "Nobody tells this to people who are beginners, I wish someone told me. All of us who do creative work, we get into it because we have good taste. But there is this gap. For the first couple years you make stuff, it's just not that good. It's trying to be good, it has potential, but it's not. But your taste, the thing that got you into the game, is still killer. And your taste is why your work disappoints you. A lot of people never get past this phase, they quit. Most people I know who do interesting, creative work went through years of this. We know our work doesn't have this special thing that we want it to have. We all go through this. And if you are just starting out or you are still in this phase, you gotta know its normal and the most important thing you can do is do a lot of work. Put yourself on a deadline so that every week you will finish one story. It is only by going through a volume of work that you will close that gap, and your work will be as good as your ambitions. And I took longer to figure out how to do this than anyone I've ever met. It's gonna take awhile. It's normal to take awhile. You've just gotta fight your way through."[27]

5 – Riding That Party Horse

I know only that what is moral is what you feel good after and what is immoral is what you feel bad after.
Ernest Hemingway

On the only road into East Glacier, Montana, off in the distance a shirtless man with long black hair wildly cascading like a ragged flag in the wind, staggered recklessly down the middle of the highway. I thought, *"Is he freakin' crazy?"* Cars swerved around the man at high speeds as he careened down the road.

My skittish wife stopped the car about a hundred feet ahead of the man. I jumped out of our rental car and anxiously waited for him like a firefighter waits to catch a person jumping from a burning building.

As the man on the road stumbled closer, I saw he was Native American, probably in his mid-20's. His body had deep gashes on it as if he had tangled with a Grizzly Bear and his arm was clearly broken in several places.

He wailed loudly, *"It f***ing hurts!"* It seemed prudent to get him out of the middle of the road and onto the shoulder. He was in no mood to cooperate so he continued obstinately on his downward path on the road into town.

After much begging and cajoling from me and another man, he finally did come to the side of the road and writhed on the ground while moaning the refrain that his arm *"F***ing hurts."*

As we came face-to-face, it was clear that he was completely inebriated. From what we were able to piece together, the man had been thrown from his horse while drunk riding in the nearby mountains. We called 9-1-1.

Soon, a local Sheriff arrived on the scene and nonchalantly asked the drunken and damaged man what had happened, saying something like *"What's up, Bud?"* This seemed routine as writing a parking ticket. The Sheriff dismissed us and soon an ambulance ambled through town taking this broken man to the hospital.

I assume that this Native American man didn't normally have problems riding his horse in the mountains being that he probably grew up riding. But adding alcohol abuse to the experience made it quite dangerous and damaging. Alcohol abuse in Native American communities is an epidemic.

This is much like what can happen to college students riding the *"Party Horse."* Some students can't envision a life in college without the Party Horse. They figure saddling up and riding with the crowd is better than walking alone. So they get thrown into the chaos and brokenness; what looked like fun becomes fracturing. The fact that alcohol abuse and the associated negative consequences ruin many a college career is indisputable. However, it is important to separate fact from fiction. A majority of college students aren't that reckless.

According to the Center for Science in the Public Interest, 44% of students attending 4-year colleges drink alcohol at the binge level or greater. Binge drinking is defined as the concentration (BAC) of 0.08 or above. For a typical adult, this corresponds to consuming 5 or more drinks (male) or 4 or more drinks (female) in about 2 hours.

Doing the math, that means 56% of college students either drink in moderation (not to get drunk) or do not drink at all. That probably is a surprising statistic for some. Many college-bound students assume that there is no alternative to the Party Horse and all are riding it. Not so.

A researcher by the name of H. Wesley Perkins, who has studied college student and alcohol extensively, notes, "What research shows is that students tend to grossly misperceive their peer norms when it comes to alcohol use. That's not to say that there aren't problems with alcohol use on campus. There are a number of students who drink at high-risk levels, but the majority don't; binge drinking is not the norm even though it's overwhelmingly perceived as being the norm.

What becomes important are the factors driving risky behaviors and problem drinking in college populations. Are the actual norms influencing behavior, or is it just students' perceptions of the norms that affect behavior?"[28]

College should be an adventure but please don't blindly imbibe the concoction that insists that alcohol is a necessity in order to enjoy the journey. John Belushi, the lead actor in the iconic college film *Animal House*, died because of a drug overdose. My first roommate in college killed himself while driving intoxicated. Tragedies, either large or small, come from too much alcohol and other substance abuse. No one starts drinking wanting to become an alcoholic but millions are or are in recovery. So, what can you do instead of getting roaring drunk at night and wretchedly sick in the morning while attending college? Ken Procaccianti, for StudentAdvisor.com, in his essay *"Fun Things to Do in College That Don't Involve Drinking"*[29] tells his story:

"I entered college as a member of the men's soccer team. An injury in my sophomore year then derailed my athletic aspirations, and without two-a-days on my schedule, I suddenly had a lot of free time.

I was instantly struck by what seemed like a huge void of fun stuff to do around campus for people like me who didn't want to get sloshed every night. Soon thereafter, I started Hammered.org to showcase the many ways to have a good time without alcohol and other drugs. Rather than preach to fellow students, Hammered.org demonstrates that you can have fun without booze for one night of your weekend, your entire life, or anytime in between. Here's how you can have fun without drinking:

Free is Good

Don't rule out an event because it is free. On Hammered.org, we often highlight free festivals, concerts, fairs, movie screenings and a lot more. Not only will you have a great time, it'll cost you less than a Natty Ice.

Fun, Out of the Ordinary, and Sometimes Offbeat

Keep it interesting. Check out the local independent movie theatre's midnight shows. Look for free student admission at local museums. Eat some good food at international cultural festivals. Flash mobs may have jumped the shark, but keep your eye out anyway for some impromptu public shenanigans.

Be a Tourist

Be a tourist in your own city, minus the fanny pack and fold-out map. You're most likely living in a new place. Check it out. See the sights. Do all the touristy stuff. Don't take it for granted because four years from now, someone from back home will ask, *"How is that <insert major landmark>?"* and you won't have an answer."

Campus Philly, a consortium of colleges in the Philadelphia Metro Area which enroll a quarter million college students (www.campusphilly.org), promotes hundreds of events and experiences yearly, and most of them can be enjoyed without alcohol. If you can't find something to do without booze and beer, you are just not looking.

EDGE IDEA: It is possible to have a wild ride of experiences in college without using and abusing alcohol. If you are going to drink, at least wait until you are 21 when you may have more maturity to not get thrown from the Party Horse.

6 – Roman Candle Relationships

The only people for me are the mad ones, the ones who are mad to live, mad to talk, mad to be saved, desirous of everything at the same time, the ones who never yawn or say a commonplace thing, but burn, burn, burn, like fabulous yellow roman candles exploding like spiders across the stars and in the middle you see the blue centerlight and everybody goes "Awww!"
Jack Kerouac

The Mad, Mad Trip to the Top of Two Medicine...
And Beyond

On the trail to the Top of Two Medicine Pass, we had a suspicion we might have some company. Warm, blue bear scat (excrement) steaming like a bowl of porridge in the cool morning air, was served up on the dirt before us. It was bluish in color from all of the huckleberries the bear had recently eaten getting ready for hibernation. One bear can consume over 100,000 huckleberries a day as she prepares for a long winter's nap. Ten minutes later we came upon a second threatening pile even warmer and bluer than the first pile. Seeing a Grizzly up close now didn't seem quite as appealing. I imagined the hot breath of a Grizz on my neck moments before she clawed me to death. We pressed on. Soon, we met a scared and alone veteran hiker coming down the trail who had decided to turn around after seeing the second pile and reconsidering the hike a few minutes later. We convinced her to join us on the hike to the top of the mountain. *"Fear Not,"* I preached to myself as I carefully re-read the directions of operation on the side of the mace spray can. Armed with mace all-around we went on our way and conquered the mountain.

EDGE IDEA: Traveling with others who have the same goals enhances courage and perseverance.

Later that evening we joined her, her daughter, and her daughter's husband at one of the few restaurants in town, a Mexican food joint called El Serranos. Little did I know that what awaited me there were not only some delicious enchiladas and quenching cold beer, but an invitation to share my passion for the college transition the next day with Native American high school students. Wow!

You see, the daughter's husband was a teacher at Blackfeet Academy. He was so excited by my experiences and expertise that he invited me out to speak to his students. I immediately accepted the offer. Blackfeet Academy is a school for Native American teens who have dropped out and then decided to come back to earn a high school diploma. Up until then, I had zero experience interacting with Native American youth, so I could hardly contain my enthusiasm. Like the night before Christmas when I was a kid.

Officially Leaving the Comfort Zone and Into the Unknown Classroom

The Reservation in Browning, Montana for the Blackfeet Tribe is a place of sadness. Listless packs of dogs roam the streets aimlessly, houses stand in a state of disrepair, rusty cars creak down the streets, and many of the Native People look beaten down by life. It is a hard place to grow up because of the hopelessness that many of the young people feel.

Alcoholism, crime, abuse, single-parent families, unemployment, and other scourges stalk the place like wolves. I wasn't entirely naive about these sad realities driving in but it did become much more real when I saw it firsthand.

How hopeless? Suicide rates for Native American adolescents are astronomically high as compared to other youth. "In the Great Plains, the area west of the Mississippi River and east of the Rocky Mountains which includes the states of South Dakota, Wyoming, Montana, Nebraska, Colorado, Kansas, New Mexico, Oklahoma, Texas, and my state of North Dakota, the youth suicide rate has reached epidemic proportions. On certain reservations, the incidence of youth suicide has been documented at 10 times the national average." Senator Byron L. Dorgan (D-ND).

As I prepared for the college transition talk, I pondered how my presentation might apply to the world of these Native American students. What unique challenges were they facing? Further, I really wondered if I could really bring lasting hope to these young people.

As an educator I firmly believe what Nelson Mandela, the anti-apartheid activist from South Africa unjustly imprisoned by the Afrikaner regime for 27 years, said "Education is the most powerful weapon which you can use to change the world."[30]

Mandela's autobiography *Long Walk to Freedom* details his life starting out a boy in a small dusty African village, to his schooling and becoming an attorney, his activism in the African National Congress, to his long and hard nearly three decades in prison for opposing an unjust government, and then finally becoming president of South Africa. Education is the door out of oppression into opportunity. I came to the class wanting to impart this vision.

I was so stoked before the presentation that I contemplated not drinking coffee that morning because the adrenaline was already pumping without the caffeine. I decided to drink only half a cup so that I wouldn't be bouncing off the ceiling like some crazed Two Medicine Mountain man. When entering the class all eyes were on me. I sensed that the teens were intrigued but skeptical. *"Who is this tall white dude?"* was the thought that seemed to be in the air. I think they were impressed that I was on vacation and still decided to come to their class.

After a brief introduction I distributed the college transition hand-out, and began the talk. After I started, a frazzled girl rushed into the classroom and apologized for being late and interrupting my talk. She said that her baby was sick and she couldn't find anyone to take care of her.

I learned that many of the students were not consistently being encouraged to go to college by their parents and community. The school was the one place where they heard that education equals opportunity. One thoughtful young man mentioned that he was very concerned that if he went to college, which would be populated mostly by white students, faculty, and administration, that he would lose his culture. Several other students seconded his observation.

There did seem to be a prevailing spirit of ambivalence in the room underlying the students' reaction, not necessarily to me, but just in general. *"We have been betrayed before"* seemed to be the unspoken message. And based on the history of how Native Americans have been treated, that should not have been surprising.

When I came to the alcohol and party scene part of the presentation about mid-way through, I mentioned the drunken Native American man with the broken arm incident from the previous day. The students commented that it was no big deal; that stuff like that happened all of the time. A big extroverted young man who looked to be a leader in the class commented nonchalantly that this incident was nothing to be shocked about.

Alcohol abuse seemed to be apathetically accepted rather than being confronted and challenged. Apathy is often the response of people who feel as if their choices don't matter, don't feel in control, and this story of the drunken Native American man was an example of this par excellence. I considered that maybe the students had learned to not care too much because they didn't feel like they have any real choices to improve upon their lives.

College does not seem to be within their grasp. Moreover if they did go to college, would they trade their identity and culture? It is possible to be educated and not lose one's cultural identity but it takes courage and commitment to not go along to get along.

At that point in my talk, I felt deep anguish. I shared with the students how abnormal it was having cars going 60 mph, dodging a drunken man with a broken body staggering down the middle of a major highway, swerving around him like he was some moving piece of garbage.

I challenged the class that their apathy, understandable for sure, was now part of the problem. I desperately wanted to get the students unstuck and wasn't going to miss the opportunity to light a fire.

The school counselor, a Native American young woman, who had gone to college for a undergraduate degree and then to Harvard for her Master's and then decided to come back to the Reservation to make a difference, embraced my message. After the talk, I pointed to her as a role model and let the kids know that she could have gone anywhere and been hired for a position and she made a decision to return to her people. True excellence by example is hard to ignore.

After my presentation concluded, I was spent-- I felt like I was in a fight for them and for their souls and consciences--one of the students quietly asked if I would be coming back again. It broke my heart to say, *"Probably not."* Better to not make promises than to break promises.

I was encouraged because he clearly was expressing a desire for more of what I had offered that day. I gave a damn and perhaps it gave him and the other students the courage and confidence to give a damn too.

As we pulled out of the Blackfeet Academy parking lot, a girl who had been in the classroom smiled and kindly waved good-bye. I had taken some risks with my talk and the student and staff appreciation was all the reward I needed.

As a parting gift, the students gave me some Sweet Grass to burn (like incense). Once this book is published, I am firing it up!

What If?

What if my wife and I decided to not go on a vacation to Montana?

What if we decided to not climb Two Medicine the day before?

What if we turned around when we saw the bear scat? The first time?

What if we turned immediately around after seeing the second pile of bear scat?

What if we didn't invite the woman hiker to join us to the top?

What if she declined our offer?

What if we decided to not have dinner with her family?

What if the teacher had not asked me to speak?

What if I declined the opportunity to talk to the Native American students?

What if I decided to play it safe in the class room and not light a fire?

This classroom interaction would never have happened unless we had left our comfort zone. This experience with the Native American kids was by far the highlight of my vacation and one of the best experiences of my life.

David Brooks in his essay, *"The Haimish Line"*, writes, "We live in a highly individualistic culture. When we're shopping for a vacation we're primarily thinking about Where. The travel companies offer brochures showing private beaches and phenomenal sights. But when you come back from vacation, you primarily treasure the memories of Who--the people you met from faraway places, and the lives you came in contact with...buy experiences instead of things." [31]

I treasure this experience because I deeply treasured the Native American teenagers. I think they knew this.

The Moral of the Story

Here is the take away lesson: It always confounds me to hear of college students paying thousands of dollars for college per semester but then they spend a good deal of time doing activities that they could do anywhere for a lot less money like play video games for hours in the dorm or drinking booze. It is like playing around with sparklers on July 4th in your backyard alone when a world-class firework festival was within a short drive. You have one this one precious opportunity to explode in college, to grow, to be in the words of Kerouac, to be "mad."

Kerouac in his book *Dharma Bums* penned, "Colleges being nothing but grooming schools for the middle class non-identity which usually finds its perfect expression on the outskirts of the campus in rows of well-to-do houses with lawns and television sets each living room with everybody looking at the same thing and thinking the same thing at the same time while the Japhies of the world go prowling in the wilderness to hear the voice crying in the wilderness, to find the ecstasy of the stars, to find the dark mysterious secret of the origin of faceless wonderless crapulous civilization."

Safe suburban TV watching sparklers versus in person world-changing fireworks. The 'burbs don't have to be starless and sterile places of the same sub-divisions, strip malls, shopping centers, and schools, no matter where you live in the U.S., but they look numbingly similar.

Musician Derek Sivers, who built an online business called CDBaby for unsigned bands to sell their music, and then later sold the company for 13 million dollars, has written a book called *Anything You Want*[32] where he details quite entertainingly his path to success with CDBaby.

He writes about good decisions that he made as well as serious missteps along the way. At the conclusion of the book he invites readers to email him and ask him a question or just to say "hi."

So I emailed him and asked him the question, *"What is the one thing that you would share with to-be college students?"*

Here is what he wrote back: (excerpted from his blog essay *"My Best Advice for Students."*)

"Looking back, my only Berklee (a college for musicians) classmates that got successful were the ones who were fiercely focused, determined, and undistractable.... If you want to be above average, you must push yourself to do more than required...there's a martial arts saying, "When you are not practicing, someone else is. When you meet him, he will win.

So I came back to Berklee with gusto. I decided to squeeze every bit of knowledge out of this place. Nobody was going to do it for me...Money is nothing more than neutral proof that you're adding value to people's lives. Making sure you're making money is just a way of making sure you're doing something of value to others. Remember that this usually comes from doing the things that most people don't do.

For example: How much does the world pay people to play video games? Nothing, because everyone does it. How much does the world pay people to make video games? A ton, because very few can do it, and lots of people want it.

Be one of the few that has the guts to do something shocking. Be one of the few that takes your lessons here as a starting point, and pushes yourself to do more with what you learn. Be one of the few that knows how to help yourself, instead of expecting others to do it for you. Be one of the few that does much more than is required.

And most importantly, be one of the few that stays in the shed to practice, while everyone else is surfing the net, flirting on MySpace (the quote was from 2008), and watching TV."[33]

Check out this video on YouTube of these thoughts: http://www.youtube.com/watch?v=gxYt--CFXK0

He offered this final piece of advice: "I have an easy rule-of-thumb to follow:

Whatever excites you, go do it.
Whatever scares you, go do it.

Every time you're making a choice, one choice is the safe/comfortable choice--and one choice is the risky/uncomfortable choice. The risky/uncomfortable choice is the one that will teach you the most and make you grow the most, so that's the one you should choose." I would modify the statement to "usually." There are dumb risks.

However, The Terrible Risk of Not Taking Risks

I conversed with an elderly man at a Visitors Center in Glacier National Park. He looked to be about 75 and walked with a cane. His wispy thin silver hair was ruffled and scattered by the wind like a breeze through an October Iowa wheat field around harvest.

The bright autumnal sun reflected off his glasses. It was one of those conversations that probably lasted less than sixty seconds, but it seemed like it lasted a day. I am not even sure how or why the profound conversation started. I was planning going to the restroom and make a quick pass through the Visitors Center at St. Mary's before we set off on the Going-to-the-Sun Road and hiking up into the high mountains to the glaciers.

He sadly told me that he was too old and infirmed to do anything physical but take a short walk to the restroom. He was going to have to miss walking the majestic mountains. He would have to stay in his car and tour the park by automobile. Chances are that he would miss most of the sights--the roaring waterfalls, the pure deep blue lakes, the craggy cliffs, the wildlife, and the ancient glaciers.

He lamented that he could have visited Glacier National Park when he was younger. He added sorrowfully that Glacier National Park was only a couple of days away by car from where he lived his whole life. He could and should have come here sooner he said.

"Regret for the things we did can be tempered by time. It is regret for the things that we did not do that is inconsolable." (Sidney J. Harris)

EDGE IDEA: Apathy is quiet but deadly, like a silencer on a revolver. Or, as Bono from U2 states, "It's stasis that kills you off in the end, not ambition."

Tim Dalrymple states wisely and winsomely, "The transition to college offers extraordinary opportunities to improve your character and enrich your personality. Commit, for your first year, to try something new every week. Go to a Taiko concert, write a piece for the school newspaper, watch an obscure foreign film, sign up for that sailing (or golf or Swahili or classical guitar) class, attend that public lecture (public lectures are among the most powerful and the most underutilized resources you can tap at college), go bungee jumping or apply for overseas study in Europe or a research trip to the Amazon.

Countless students can attest that the most important things they did in college took place outside the classroom. If you're faithful with your classes, you'll receive your education and training. But if you're faithful with the other opportunities college affords you, your horizons, your sensibilities, your sense of yourself and your world will expand exponentially."[34]

There are many avenues towards involvement socially in college such as intramural sports, the arts and theatre, in department-related organizations such as business, newspaper, radio station, TV broadcasting, part-time work-study jobs, and a myriad of informal opportunities to interact with others. You will never really learn much about yourself by staring at an Xbox screen all day.

It is only when you put yourself out into the social river that you learn to ride the relational rapids. Rather than spread yourself thin, select one or two extracurricular activities and go deep. Get beyond the surface and don't skip around like a smooth rock on a lake.

You should look to Clubs that are primarily run by students who have a deep commitment to be change agents; that perhaps are even a bit controversial. It has been my experience that too many organizations tend to be run by conventional types who drain the energy, mission, and creativity out of groups. Or, even start your own Club.

Forge connections with like-minded peers, follow the protocols to get approved by the college's administration, get creative, cut loose, and let it rip. Or keep it off the books to retain autonomy. Do something monumental. Learn from each other, critique each others' work constructively, and step up.

Reed College in Oregon is a quirky offbeat school. Their offerings of Clubs look like a delicious array of opportunities to get active and serve. To leave your old sparkler self behind and becoming the colorful firework exploding away from the safety and security of the ground and into the enormous sky.

Here is a menu of some of the more interesting Clubs (A-Z):

ARG (Association of Reed Gamers). Some gaming is fine.

BISON BISON (Beedle dee, dee dee dee, two ladies)...(My Note: *I have no idea what this is about but thought it hilarious)*

Chimes of Mora (pianos, strings, and multiple page turners, *Lord of the Rings* music)

DxOxTxUx (defending the universe)

Ecuador Service Project (do service work in indigenous communities in the Andes)

Fluffy Sheep Knit Collective (learn to knit)

Greenboard (student environmental collective concerned about climate change)

History Club (history is badass)

Ice Cream Society (make ice cream from scratch)

Kenjutsu (learn sword techniques of feudal Japan)

La Casa Hispana (flamenco dancing, soccer, Latin music, Argentinean cuisine)

Men's Ultimate (Frisbee game with tournaments in the Northwest)

New York Times on Campus (reading the N.Y. Times daily in the Commons)

Oh For Christ's Sake (come for the brownies, stay for Jesus)

Print Shoppe (make cool sh*t)

Reed Talks (organizes awesome conferences and events on the Reed campus)

Skatepark Adventure Club (adventure abounds)

Tool Kollective (provides the tools necessary to complete a project)

Uncommons (a cooking organization comprised of students who are passionate about making good food)

Weapons of Mass Distraction (teaches circus skills)

See the full offerings:

http://www.reed.edu/student_activities/student_org_search/index.php?submit=Search

Reed's website states, "Reed graduates earning doctorates or winning postgraduate fellowships and scholarships (such as Rhodes, Fulbright, Watson, and Mellon) at rates higher than all but a handful of other colleges."

Says Reed President Diver, "Reed is a paradigmatic example of a college committed--and committed solely--to the cultivation of a thirst for knowledge. Reed illustrates a relatively small, but robust, segment of higher education whose virtues may not always be celebrated by the popular press, but can still be found by those who truly seek them."

That thirst is not just cultivated in the classroom but throughout the totality of the college experience. The Club culture, cultivates this thirst.

And, you only want to play video games? SHEESH!

7 - Big Sky College

Standing under the Big Sky I feel free.
A.B. Guthrie

Montana is popularly known as *"Big Sky Country."* Outside of Alaska it is the wildest state in the Union. When development occurs it is in limited spaces of high concentration. Otherwise, it is open land with endless mountains and big skies. At night, due to the lack of surface light from cities and suburbia, the stars in the sky--the face of the Universe--appears.

Mere words cannot explain the fantastic and wondrous display. It made me feel small, as well it should. I could see how the ancients in their tales of the Zodiac sought to capture the wonder of looking up and the effect it had on them internally, thus provoking questions about the meaning of life.

In this book thus far, I have identified key collegiate constellations:

Don't let your past define you.

Your imagination is critical to envisioning your future.

Organizing your time is the way of establishing priorities and defining goals.
Learning is intrinsically rewarding, far surpassing just the grade.

Knowledge should inculcate wisdom and a sense of humility.

Your passions are a big clue about your vocational purpose.

Recognizing that college is a unique social opportunity which is to be appreciated and not wasted.

Pushing your limits and extending your boundaries by taking risks.

Just as in the evening sky, such remarkable constellations exist in your Big Sky of college. Yet, sometimes in order to see them in their totality, you must step out of the glare of the crowds by day and contemplate such things at night.

Contemplation

Tim Cook, in his review of Andrew Delabanco's book *College: What It Is, And Should Be*, writes, "All students deserve something more from college than semi-supervised fun or the services of an employment ~ency." Delabanco decries students "Scarcely have ᵉ for... contemplation; they should have the ₁us chance to think and reflect before life engulfs ᵓ5

ᵉ best way to accomplish this is to escape the ᵗnd well-lit college campus into the woods, ᵉaches, or other secluded spaces, and ₑᵍht Big Sky.

ᵗid Thoreau in his book *Walden, or* ᵛrote about the truly restoring ᵗss: "We need the tonic of ᵗ have enough of nature. We ᵗimits transgressed, and ᵗhere we never wander."

We must have our Waldens, if only for a day or two. To think, to reflect.

When Wisconsin native Justin Vernon of the band Bon Iver (Bon-Ee-Ver, the name is a play on the words that mean *"Good Winter"* in French) composed and recorded his critically acclaimed album *For Emma, Forever Ago*, he was encamped in his Dad's cabin in the Wisconsin woods for three snowy winter months.

He was badly bruised artistically from his band falling apart, emotionally licking his wounds from a jarring romantic break-up, and physically recuperating from mononucleosis. He is quoted as saying "I went there from North Carolina because I didn't know where else to go and I knew that I wanted to be alone and I knew that I wanted to be where it was cold."[36]

He observed, "The record was me finally stopping a terrible, slow spin that had been building for years. Me alleviating memories, confronting a lot of lost love, longing and mediocrity." [37] "There is nothing like heartache", in the words of rock journalist Lizzie Goodman, "to inspire great art."

In a *New York Times* article about Vernon, the piece notes:

"For college, Vernon stayed close to home, attending the Eau Claire campus of the University of Wisconsin, which has one of the most well regarded jazz studies programs in the country. By this time he was playing in a string of bands--first came Mount Vernon, a jazz-minded party band with as many as 10 members, one of whom was Sara Jensen, a saxophonist who was Vernon's first love. In so much as the Emma of the first album is a person--Vernon says that *"Emma"* is *"a place, an idea that you get hung up on"*--it's Jensen. They broke up midway through college, but they have remained close.

Vernon played guitar, one of the less demanding instruments in a jazz environment. A religion major, he tried studying music theory, but it didn't feel right. *"I didn't want to be proficient,"* he said. *"It seemed like other people were valuing things that were more about technical ability and not, like, feel."*[38]

EDGE IDEA: College is a place to unite head and heart, fact and feeling.

At the end of his band's performance on the PBS show *Austin City Limits*, Vernon reflected on the cabin experience--that he needed to touch down, not open his mouth for days to speak, stop editing himself, drop the mirror he wore in relating and reacting to others, and feel peace. And he created a musical masterpiece, with an initial run of 500 CDs that has touched thousands. At last count, the album has gone gold and sold over 500,000 copies.

"Bon Iver", Vernon said, is "a sentiment" more than a music project and it connected. Vernon is regularly approached by fans who tell him how his music healed them. "It's just always weird to hear people talk to me about this," he said, "Because it's like: 'Yeah, I know. It did that to me too.' "[39] The self-released record got a rave review from *Pitchfork*, which helped lead to Bon Iver's association with the independent record label *Jagjaguwar*, based in Bloomington, Ind. It was on dozens of 2008 year-end lists.

In the song *"Woods"* Vernon sings "I'm up in the woods, I'm down on my mind, I'm building a still, to slow down the time."

Create Your Own Alone Album

Get away from the excitement and chaos of campus, to a secluded space during the semester for a weekend or two. This is often the best way to create opportunities for reflection. You can go alone or with a small group of no-drama friends.

Wild road trips are great for open-ended experiences where anything can happen and I emphatically encourage that you do these throughout your college years--my buddies and I made a legendary 24 hour visit to New York City in college to the *Crack-Down Concert* that was amazing--but they are rarely resting. Likewise, going on retreats with hundreds of people is fantastic but not soul-restoring.

How you restore yourself can also be a trait of your personality. Extroverts tend to be recharged by crowds and introverts tend to be drained by crowds. Yet, even extroverts need to turn inward on occasion. Try to also take one day a week off from school work, and work in general. It will do your body, mind, and soul good.

EDGE IDEA*:* Unplug from your smart phone, the computer, social media, the TV/music, and the campus social scene on a regular basis. You won't die, believe me, even though the withdrawal will feel like kicking an espresso addiction.

Don't just go home and hide out in your room. Instead, find a place that provides a safe haven for thinking about what you are doing (this is more practical), and more importantly, why you are doing it (this is more philosophical).

Margaret Manning, in her essay *Spiritual Geography* writes, "In a culture that values productivity over reflection, I am reminded that the spiritual geography of wilderness serves as a necessary correction. We don't often allow ourselves to explore the barrenness of our internal wilderness."[40]

Alyssa Bryant captures this barrenness in her essay: *"The Spiritual Struggles of College Students: Illuminating a Critical Development Phenomenon"* by sharing this quote from a college student:

> *"Sometimes I feel like my struggles are just so powerful; I can't just get over them. I just feel so defeated. I have felt so lost. I felt like I had nowhere to go."*[41]

Bryant identifies the ingredients of this struggle:

What is the meaning of life?

Why are we put here?

Is there a purpose?

What will happen to us after we die?

Why do we suffer, some so much more than others?

Most college students, to one degree or another, wrestle with questions of meaning, purpose, suffering, and the existence of God. It helps if you look up, where you will see stars shining that would not have appeared unless the darkness had descended.

In Vale of The Night of Suffering: Soul Making

In his book *Lament for a Son* by Nicholas Wolterstorff, he as a father writes of the loss of his 25 year-old son Eric in a mountain-climbing accident in Europe: "In this valley of suffering, despair and bitterness are brewed. But there also character is made. The valley of suffering is the vale of soul-making."

The star Polaris, often called the North Star, is treated specially due to its proximity to the North Pole. When navigating in the northern hemisphere, strategies can be employed in reference to Polaris to determine true north.

Generations of trekkers have grasped the importance of always knowing the location of the North Star. As the only fixed point in the night sky, the North Star is a constant companion and sure reference for setting one's course. Like Truth itself, the North Star position never changes and provides direction.

In fact, American slaves used the North Star to escape from slavery, leaving the South of servitude to the North of freedom. The slaves' final goal was Canada, north of the U.S. border. Slavery was not permitted there, and American laws that allowed people to capture runaway slaves had no effect.

Three Philosophical Stars: Past, Present, & Future

Just like the North Star is used for navigation, Truth also guides us on our journey through the dark night.

THE TRUTH OF OUR PAST: *"We must not wish for the disappearance of our troubles but for the grace to transform them."* **Simone Weil**

Reflect on your past trials. What have you learned? What good has come from it?

THE TRUTH OF OUR PRESENT: *"Change your life today. Don't gamble on the future, act now, without delay."* **Simone de Beauvoir**

What can you do today to move forward? Progress is always possible.

THE TRUTH OF OUR FUTURE *"Life can only be understood backwards; but it must be lived forwards."* **Søren Kierkegaard**

Rather than fear the future, accept that it is ultimately unknowable. Embrace the adventure.

I was planning to be a basketball star in college and then in the NBA but my bad left knee ended that plan. So, I redirected my energy and started to write seriously, which eventually resulted in earning a Ph.D. and writing this book.

EDGE IDEA: Broken dreams sometimes lead to better dreams.

Check out some more of my thoughts at the following blog address:

http://bierkergaard.blogspot.com

Make Your Life Extraordinary

Maybe you have seen the film *Dead Poets Society* about a teacher and a group of young high school aged men. The new English teacher, Mr. Keating, gets them to grasp that they must make the most of their days. The young men form a secret society to read great works of literature in a cave off-campus at night.

Although the story has a tragic end, it still shines as a work of inspiration. On one of the first days of class, Mr. Keating tells his students to follow him out into a hallowed hall where photographs of prior students are on display.

He tells them:

"They're not that different from you, are they? Same haircuts. Full of hormones, just like you. Invincible, just like you feel. The world is their oyster. They believe they're destined for great things, just like many of you, their eyes are full of hope, just like you. Did they wait until it was too late to make from their lives even one iota of what they were capable?

Because, you see gentlemen, these boys are now fertilizing daffodils. But if you listen real close, you can hear them whisper their legacy to you. Go on, lean in. Listen, you hear it?- - Carpe--hear it?--Carpe, Carpe Diem, seize the day boys, make your lives extraordinary." Make your college years extraordinary.

The Final Step in Our Journey

As McKay Jenkins notes in his book *White Death*, after seven failed tries, the British climber

80

Edward Whymper and seven on his team were the first to climb the Matterhorn in the Alps in 1865 and became famous. On the descent, though, Whymper looked on helplessly as four members of his team fell to their deaths off of a 4,000 foot precipice. Half made it back.

Whymper wrote of his triumphs and tragedies in the mountains, "There have been joys too great to describe in words, and there have been griefs upon which I have not dared to dwell; and with these in mind I say: Climb if you will, but remember that courage and strength are naught without prudence, and that a momentary negligence may destroy the happiness of a lifetime. Do nothing in haste; look well to each step; and from the beginning think what may be the end."

Will you come with me to the mountains? It will hurt at first, until your feet are hardened. Reality is harsh to the feet of shadows. But will you come?

C.S. Lewis, *The Great Divorce*

On the Edge in Glacier National Park, Montana

Album: Into The Wild
Lyrics/ Music: Ed Vedder

SETTING FORTH

Be it, no concern
Point of no return
Go forward in reverse
This I will recall
Yeah, every time I fall

Ahh-oohhh setting forth in the universe
Ahh-oohhh setting forth in the universe

Acknowledgements

I would truly be remiss if I did not thank the people below. They all have helped me become who I am and played a role in this book. Mr. James Craney, the best English teacher ever. Ray Carr and Tony Miles, my bosses at Glen Mills Schools. Brother Rob Paire, Steve Becker, Troy Jackson, and Todd Klick--who has consistently taught me how to dream by his own example. Dr. Joyce Smedley, Counselor Education professor at Millersville University. Glenn Snelbecker, William Fullard, and Joe DuCette, professors in the Ed. Psych program at Temple University. Go Owls! The Northeastern School District community, especially Kris Hach, Bethany Gamber, Jennifer Bisignani, and Wanda Salisbury, fellow Guidance Department colleagues...and of course the students. My funky and fiercely loyal Bierker family. Jennifer Brown, for the wonderful art work on the cover. Matt Lester, a photographer of all things college. Sean Rajnic, for his support. VERITAS. Tom Becker/The Rowhouse. The Lancast. Eugene Peterson for his kind words and encouragement at the book's start. The students and staff at Blackfeet Academy. PACE and Upward Bound students and staff at Millersville University circa 1989-1991. I would also like to personally thank these five individuals who read and reviewed this book in its various seasons of growth and helped me hack it down to size, cut it into shape, assemble the words as wood, sand it smooth, and put on the finishing varnish: Lina, Tim Shea, Mike Pollis, Byron Borger, and George Bierker. Each of you had an angle on the book that helped the construction immensely.

The book is roughly hewn. I trust that any remaining flaws give it character and shows that something can be quite good even if it ain't perfect. Sorry that the editing was so punishing.

Lastly, gratitude to C.S. Lewis, whose book *"God In The Dock"* opened my eyes and filled my soul with writing that was both true and beautiful. As he wrote, "Hardships often prepare ordinary people for an extraordinary destiny."

Endnotes

[1] McKay, Jenkins. *The White Death,* 2001. New York: Random House. Print.

[2] Bittle, Scott. "The Third Rail Question on College." *www.publicagenda.org.* Public Agenda, 2010. Web. September 13, 2013.

[3] "Glossary of Rock, Ice, and Mountain Climbing Terms." *www.santiamalpineclub.org.* Santiam Alpine Club, 2013 Web. 13 September, 2013.

[4] Bernbaum, Edwin. "Peak Paradigms: Mountain Metaphors of Leadership and Teamwork." *leadership.wharton.upenn. edu,* 2008. Web. 13 September, 2013.

[5] "2009 Ahern Pass Tragedy" *www.summitpost.org.* SummitPost.org, 2009. Web. 13 September, 2013.

[6] Gallagher, Billy. "Cory Booker Delivers 2012 Commencement Address." *www.stanforddaily.com* The Stanford Daily, 2012. Web. 13 September, 2013.

[7] Batterson, Mark. "Extreme Faith." *http://forum.theaterchurch.com.* National Community Church, 2003. Web. 13 September, 2013.

[8] Stibel, Jeff. "Why I Hire People Who Fail." *http:blogs.hbr.org.* Harvard Business Review, 2011. Web. 13 September, 2013.

[9] Rowling, J.K. "The Fringe Benefits of Failure and the Importance of the Imagination." *http:newsharvard.edu/gazette.* Harvard Gazette. 2008. Web. 13 September, 2013.

[10] Money, J. "I Went to College and All I Got Was This $200,00 Bill."*www.budgetaresexy.com.* Budgets Are Sexy, 2011. Web. 13 September, 2013

[11] Quotes from Everest. *http://www.mnteverest.net/quote.html.* Web. 3 September, 2013

[12] Batterson, Mark. "Looking Foolish." *www.identitynetwork.org.* Web. 13 September, 2013

[13] Demas, Susan "The Benefits of Going to College." *www.eduguide.org.* EduGuide, 2006. Web. 13 September, 2013.

[14] Hilton, James. *Lost Horizon.* 1st Edition. New York: William Morrow and Company, 1933. Print.

[15] Podhorertz, Norman, and Green, Ashbel (Ed). *My Columbia: Reminiscences of University Life.* New York: Columbia University, 2005. Print.

[16] LaPorte, Danielle. *The Firestarter Sessions.* New York: Random House, 2012. Print.

[17] Rowling, J.K. "The Fringe Benefits of Failure and the Importance of the Imagination." *http:newsharvard.edu/gazette.* Harvard Gazette. 2008. Web. 13 September, 2013.

[18] Wikipedia http://en.wikipedia.org/wiki/Pierian_Spring. Web. 15 February 2014

[19] Dalyrymple, Tim. "An Open Letter to a College Freshman." *http://www.patheos.com/blogs/philosophicalfragments.* September 1, 2011. Web. 21 Sept. 2013.

[20] Rogers, Fred. "Quotes of Fred Rogers." *www.goodreads.com.* Web. 21 Sept. 2013.

[21] Gallo, Carmine. "Homeless Man Turned Millionaire Offers the Best Advice I Ever Got." *www.forbes.com.* 2011. Web. 28 Sept. 2013.

[22] Donnelly, Tim. "10 Tips on Hiring For Creativity." *www.inc.com.* 2011. Web. 28 Sept. 2013.

[23] Godin, Seth. *Tribes.* New York: Penguin, 2008. Print.

[24] Wolf, Gary, "Steve Jobs: The Next Insanely Great Thing." *Wired* December 2006. Print. http://www.wired.com/wired/archive/4.02/jobs_pr.html Web.28 September 2013

[25] Isaacson, Walter. "Steve Jobs Biographer." *http://archive.feedblitz.com/600132/~4089667.* Fast Company, 2012. Web. 28 September 2013.

[26] Glancey, Jonathan. "Steve Jobs: iDesigned Your Life." *www.theguardian.com.* The Guardian, 2011. Web. 28 September 2013.

[27] Glass, Ira. http://www.goodreads.com/quotes/309485-nobody-tells-this-to-people-who-are-beginners-i-wish *Web.* 28 September 2013.

[28] Perkins, H. Wesley. "A Social Norms Approach to College Drinking." *www.mystudentbody.com.* 28 Sept. 2013

[29] Procaccianti, Ken. "Fun Things To Do In College That Don't Involve Drinking." *www.studentadvisor.com.* 16 Sept 2011. Web. 28 September 2013.

[30] Mandela, Nelson. "Education for All." *http://www.un.org/en/globalissues/briefingpapers/efa/quotes.shtml.* United Nations. 2013. 5 October 2013

[31] Brooks, David. "The Haimish Line." *http://www.nytimes.com/2011/08/30/opinion/brooks-the-haimish-line.html?_r=0.* The New York Times, 2011. 5 October 2013

[32] Silvers, Derek. *Anything You Want.* The Domino Project/Amazon. 2011. Ebook

[33] Silvers, Derek. "My Best Advice for Students." http://sivers.org/blog. 5 October 2013

[34] Dalyrymple, Tim. "An Open Letter to a College Freshman." *http://www.patheos.com/blogs/philosophicalfragments* September 1, 2011. Web. 5 October 2013.

[35] Delbanco, Andrew. *College: What It Was, Is, and Should Be.* Princeton: Princeton University Press, 2012. Print.

[36] *"Bon Iver."* http://www.youtube.com/watch?v=qxkn0UScF_E. Web. 19 October 2013

[37] Bon Iver. "For Emma-Bon Iver." *www.songfacts.com.* Song Facts. Web. 19 October 2013

[38] Caramanica, Jon. "Who, What, and Where Is Bon Iver?" *New York Times Magazine.* 3 June 2011. Web. 19 October 2013.

[39] Caramanica, Jon. "Who, What, and Where Is Bon Iver?" *New York Times Magazine.* 3 June 2011. Web. 19 October 2013.

[40] Manning, Margaret. "Spiritual Geography." *www.rzim.org.* Ravi Zacharias International Ministries, 2012. Web. 19 October 2012.

[41] Bryant, Alyssa. "The Spiritual Struggles of College Students." *Spirituality In Higher Education.* October 2008, 1-7. Web. 19 October 2013.